THERE'S A LION in my CORNFLAKES

Michelle Robinson   Jim Field

BLOOMSBURY
LONDON NEW DELHI NEW YORK SYDNEY

If you ever see this on a packet of cornflakes:

Ignore it!

You should see what happened when we didn't . . .

Me and my brother, Dan, made umpteen trips to the supermarket
and spent a whole year's pocket money on cereal.

It took us AGES to cut out all the coupons.

Mum was so mad she made us eat cornflakes for breakfast, lunch and tea.

She said we'd have nothing but cornflakes
until they were all gone.

That could take forever!

And she said there'd be
no more pocket money
until we'd eaten up
every last boring,
crunchy flake.

But we didn't mind.
We really wanted a free lion.

We could take it for walks.

Ride it to school.

And use it to open tin cans.*

Thursday? No lion.

Friday? No lion.

Saturday? STILL no lion.

Even worse, by the time Sunday came . . .

EVERYONE else had theirs. How unfair is that?!

Mind you, it seems everyone else had the same idea.

Poor postman.

We waited and waited for our free lion to arrive.
But there was no lion on Monday . . . or Tuesday . . . or Wednesday.

Then on Monday, a delivery truck arrived.
We were so excited!

But, one: it wasn't a lion.
Two: they sent it next door by mistake, and
three: it went ballistic in Mr Harper's back yard.

It wasn't our fault! But Mum went bonkers.
She made us apologise to Mr Harper AND tidy up.
It was awful. We had a grizzly bear, a grumpy mum
and absolutely NO free lion.

We wrote to the cereal people and complained.
They wrote back:

Mr Flaky
LTD

Dan and Eric
Pink House
Hilly Hill
Bookland
HG5 9TL

Dear Eric and Dan,

Sorry about the grizzly bear,
but we ran out of lions.

Please accept this crocodile
instead.

Yours Sincerely

Mr Flaky .

Mr Flaky

P.S. Handle with care.

"A crocodile?!" Dan said. "We didn't eat all those cornflakes for a cranky old crocodile!"

And guess what? The crocodile spent all its time in the bathroom, so no one else could get in.

Dad went nuts. He made us scrub the bath
while he telephoned the cereal people.
"Sorry," they said. "We'll sort it
out straight away."

KEEP
OUT

DAN'S ROOM

We asked for a LION.
NOT a grizzly bear, NOT a bathroom-hogging crocodile and . . .

. . . DEFINITELY not a whacking great gorilla.
But that's exactly what we got.
It took an immediate fancy to Dad's car.

He was not impressed.
"Right, that's it," he fumed. "Everyone in —
I'm going to give those cereal people a piece of my mind!"

The cereal people said sorry — AGAIN — but they really had run out of lions.
They said that we could keep the whacking great gorilla,
the bathroom-hogging crocodile and the very grizzly bear.
And they also gave us . . .

. . . a lifetime's supply of cornflakes.
Finally, Dad was happy. But Mum wasn't — and we certainly weren't.

You can't take a packet of cornflakes for a walk.

Cornflakes won't get you to school in style.

Can cornflakes help you open a tin of tomatoes? Not on your nelly.

But hang on a minute . . .

CHOMP

A crocodile is the meanest can-opening machine I've ever seen!

A grizzly bear can walk for miles and miles . . . and miles!

And there can't be a better way of
arriving at school than this!

So don't ever bother saving up for a lion,
it's not worth the trouble.
And besides, EVERYONE'S got one.

But a free tiger? Just imagine . . .

For my brother, Dan - M.R.
For Sandy - J.F.

Bloomsbury Publishing, London, New Delhi, New York and Sydney
First published in Great Britain in 2014 by Bloomsbury Publishing Plc
50 Bedford Square, London, WC1B 3DP

A CIP catalogue record of this book is available from the British Library

ISBN 978 1 4088 4559 2 (HB)
ISBN 978 1 4088 4560 8 (PB)
ISBN 978 1 4088 4558 5 (eBook)

1 3 5 7 9 10 8 6 4 2

Printed in China by Leo Paper Products, Heshan, Guangdong

All papers used by Bloomsbury Publishing are natural, recyclable products made from
wood grown in well-managed forests. The manufacturing processes conform
to the environmental regulations of the country of origin

www.bloomsbury.com

BLOOMSBURY is a registered trademark of Bloomsbury Publishing Plc